Twilight of Crooks

Twilight of Crooks

a novel

Mwalimu Johnnie MacViban

Bakwa Books

PO Box 30056 Yaounde

www.bakwabooks.com

ISBN: 978-1-7337526-3-3

Cover art by Dante Besong

For Bate Besong, who is inspiration galore.

You, Tityrus, lie under your spreading beech's covert, wooing the woodland Muse on slender reed, but we are leaving our country's bounds and sweet fields. We are outcasts from our country; you, Tityrus, at ease beneath the shade, teach the woods to re-echo "fair Amaryllis."

— Meliboeus in Virgil's *Eclogue I*

1

The white flag floating at City Hall said it all. With the symbol of a mango fruit in the centre of the flag, Tumaranda—the Big Mango City—was juicy, wholesome, and edible for those hungry for plunder. All roads led to Tumaranda because it was a port city and had OPEC membership. From Kabogasa, Ya Salaam, Beberati, Meyo-Belo, and Bongori, the migration shift was to the place where the action was. The oil boom had changed the demographics of the city; with the growing crime wave, and unrepentant police brutality, the city was at war with itself. There was despair. Bayangé Street was littered with shuttered debauched houses, and homeless children. Pointedly, one could feel the absence of social security. But then, what had become of the law on responsible parenthood?

The crisis meeting scheduled for Thursday afternoon at City Hall was just a piece of vaudeville. Despite the streaking Roman rays, there was no warmth. The air stood still. This was not the first time in two months that people would gather in City Hall. Everyone was there—the police commissioner for the city, the chief of the fire brigade, the chief of finance, the governor of the House of Corrections, a bunch of plainclothes men, and city hall officials.

From City Hall, you could see a picturesque detail of the city for miles on end. A flight of migratory birds flew over town giving a minute's darkness that did not spell gloom. Both the shade of grey and the present false climate portrayed another aspect of the changing times. The Tumaranda scene was congenial. People, it is said, do not care about the weather except when a storm is announced.

The meeting was going to be recorded.

A hive of excited voices greeted the mayor's arrival. Mayor Yuri Sonni—no surprise, an appointed official—was more interested in his next appointment than managing the city. His mayoral skills, undoubtedly, were low-keyed. He looked overworked and dour. He clasped his veiny hands, and later fidgeted with a Parker pen to focus as he took his seat at the head of a circular table.

"Gentlemen, listen up. I'm under fire," he said, broaching the state of insecurity with anger surging in every axon of his body. "Our city is no longer juicy. It needs security, and we're not doing enough."

The city police commissioner's hand shot up. "Mr Mayor, we have always worked as a team. To the best of my knowledge, your assertions look like an assessment of your administration. Give us the means, and we will perform!"

The mayor who had been peering into the hall came back to reality and said, "You know I have a political career before me and this city is not going to stop me."

This faintly hieratic pronouncement was rather too much for the gathering. Voices rose, objecting to the mayor's. Everyone was now on their feet, and the meeting was drawing to a dramatic finale barely twenty minutes after it started. This was surely the mirror image of a rotten system: the mayor had lost control.

It came as no surprise that this fiasco of a meeting was leaked to the press, a press which, though under harassment, was obsessed with tearing down the reputations of the high and the mighty.

Mayor Yuri Sonni, 53, was a man with a husky physique. When he spoke in his baritone voice, he did so dandy shyly. He was a perennial turncoat and a sell-out. He had picked up a reputation as a staunch supporter of the ruling Salami League Party. After a number of ruses, he had landed himself in the post of mayor. Working against the background that the art of governance was the mastery of chaos, he had quickly permeated the seamless tapestry of power by pitting his opponents against each other while relying on his friends to secure his current job, which was a sinecure.

Yuri Sonni, late that afternoon, sat behind his oak desk, unworried about the stack of files in front of him. He would process them at his own pace. He was not in a hurry. The most pressing of the files concerned the reconstruction of the Independence Driveway. Halfway through the construction, the contractors had just decamped! Sealing off that road while it was under repair was a serious headache to the city council; it had to reroute traffic to other pothole-infested arteries.

The mayor stood up and yawned. He looked tired, as if he had been working a lot. He smiled, shut the office door and left.

2

Bundu Bakasili, detective inspector for the 3rd Police Precinct, stepped into the entrance of the Sunflower Condominium as a slashing rain started to drop outside, pelting the glass door with reasonable weight. He walked up a flight of stairs to Yeelena Theodora's apartment, number 20, on the second floor, and rang twice. There was no answer. This was the second time in a week that he had found her absent from home. *Absence makes the heart grow fonder*, he thought. No fuss: he had the passkey.

Yeelena's living room was compact, with modern furniture, a cupboard, and electronic gadgets. It was an agreeable, unpretentious place whose French windows opened out onto the empty blue, since the building stood athwart the sandy beach sea. The walls were painted turquoise.

Bakasili enjoyed the safe anonymity of the house.

He made for the kitchenette, where the refrigerator held tinned foods, drinks, and vegetables. He took out a can of Coke and opened it, drinking half of its content in a single gulp.

Back into the living room, he appreciated the number of foreign flags adorning one wall. The other wall, next to the hi-fi, had xeroxed paintings of various schools hanging from it. Yeelena was, obviously, fascinated with the abstract, and cubism. Bakasili put on the radio and Santana's "Oye Como Va" came on.

It was now 4pm. Bakasili decided not to ring up Yeelena; he was getting used to not meeting her at home. His eye caught the cover of a *Glamour Out* magazine lying on the table. He picked it up.

The spread featured a tribute to a number of African queens history had produced: Abyssinia's Queen of Sheba, Songhai's Sarraounia, Kaduna's Queen Amina, Buganda's Elizabeth of Toro, the Ashanti's Gundo-Naa, and the legendary Dahomey Amazons. These women had possessed both beauty and political clout.

The radio continued with "Have You Ever Seen the Rain".

The rain was still pounding outside. Gusts of wind-whacked raindrops crashed against the glass panes on the window. Bakasili was glad to be safe inside the house, enjoying the warmth of the apartment. From the window, he could see the amount of water streaming out of the culvert. The rain disturbed his view of the beach. No way to catch sight of any night-time beach bunnies.

Hanging on a dry line on the balcony were all kinds of lingerie, still carrying the scent of detergents.

Staring at the rain through the window, he lost himself to his thoughts. Work at the Swallow Crime Squad had been topsy-turvy. With the sealing of the Cobra File, detectives needed a breather. The file had been a headache for many years. Matabali Tara aka Carlos, had been a modern-day highway robber who used the concrete urban jungle as his Sherwood Forest. He had mythologised his exploits up to Byronic level. Together with his gang, they acted like weasels, full of surprises. The Squad's modus operandi having been improved, the gang's last heist drew them into the police dragnet. In a shoot-out, Carlos was killed in a gloriously un-heroic martyrdom replete with cinema overdose.

*

Bakasili was tired of waiting. Why wasn't Yeelena back by now? He still had the magazine in his hands as he stood in front of the window, afraid to awaken ancient fears.

Theodora was a lovable woman—young, beautiful, and demure. Bakasili had met Yeelena at an international conference at the Tumaranda Ritz Hotel. She was thirty at the time, single, and an assistant to the personnel manager of Afro Cosmetics. Her nails were delicately polished, and she looked smart with her dresses that were often just below her knees. She was not one to complain unnecessarily, and they did not have any quarrels. Love had too many magic moments. Bakasili was fatuously content that both of them had never had any unfortunate run-ins. He had expected warmth here but now he was musing over life in Yeelena's apartment.

He stood up, relaxed, convinced he had a hunch better days were coming. His quick eye view landed on the glass cupboard that held a collection of books, decorations, souvenir pictures, and a woollen replica of a boa constrictor. In a fit of hunting curiosity, he was glad he was not a snake coddler. After draining the last drops of the Coke, he squashed the can into a ball and dropped it in the kitchen's trash can. He pulled out a pen from his chest pocket and wrote Yeelena a note, which he stuck on the refrigerator.

Twilight of Crooks

Meet me at the racecourse Saturday evening. Enjoyed myself in three dimensions. Easy when you tease me. Bakasili.

He stepped out of the building, and drove downtown in his Volvo convertible. At Freedom Run Boulevard, traffic moved in spurts. People went about posthaste as soon as the rain ceased. A bunch of them had reptilian stares. Some were prosaic-minded people, others were people with rapt gazes: goblins; truant and duplicitous hawkers; blackmailers; confident ramblers; sterling characters and ciphers; local retards full of existential despairs—a humdrum world where everyone was eking out a living or brewing hare-brained schemes to make fast bucks. A small man wearing wrecked jeans and a sweater passed by

21

Bakasili's car, reeking of alcohol and stale breath.

He gave the man a once-over and shook his head.

3

Bundu Bakasili was early at his desk on Monday morning. He sat down, and looked up at photos of wanted persons on the wall in front of him. These bad guys had been at large for too long. The outer office had about twelve tables, around which plainclothes officers crowded. Much talk across the tables centred on work, dreams, and other plans. The imperial typewriters competed with the chattering as these contraptions clanked, typing away police reports.

The phone rang. He picked it up.

"Hello, this is Yeelena. Can I speak with Inspector Bakasili?" she said.

"Yea, this is the man," Bakasili said. "How was your Sunday?"

"Wonderful. Hey, don't you ever leave me alone like that, you copper," Yeelena fired back in a tone that was more affable than accusatory. "You missed our date night. Stopping by the next day is no solution, you know."

"Please, do bear with me. I do understand, you know, that we live a profession of pedestrian domesticity," he tried to drum some sense into his meaning.

"Aha, work!"

"I do love you," he said. "I thirst for you."

"Don't blackmail me with love."

"You still there?" Since his wife died, he had not loved anyone else, until Yeelena. She laughed. "I love you. See you soon."

*

Bakasili fiddled with his pencil, and a few sheets of reports.

The phone rang again. This time, it was a former friend, Solo Matura—a *nouveau riche* who, through mailshot, had monopolised the sale of footwear from Morocco. The man was reporting a hit-and-run accident that had just occurred in front of one of his chain stores, King's View.

Their conversation soon turned lively, and ended with an invitation: "Be my guest for a beer at the Kennedy Club," Solo Matura said.

When the call ended, Bakasili opened the top drawer of his desk, and took out a file. A newspaper clipping from *The Tumaranda Star* stared at him from within the file. The story printed on it was about a triple murder that had been classified as a cold case. Many thought it was a crime of passion, but this did not ring true to Bakasili. He thought back to the murder, which had taken place two years ago, and felt a chill.

*

THE TUMARANDA STAR
Family Slain in Ghost Strike: Revenge Feared
by Jason Makelekele

Neighbours and passers-by were shocked as they watched the police wheel the bodies of the victims of a triple homicide out of No. 43 Palm Groove Street into an ambulance.

The victims are Mabala Mungo, 45, his wife, Nadia Mungo, 32, and their daughter, Mildred Mungo, 3. They were found early on Monday morning by their housekeeper, Magda Nufi, when she came in to work, and called the police immediately.

The coroner says the deaths occurred sometime around midnight. Speaking to the press, Chief Investigating Officer, Detective Inspector Tata N'Zambe says the murders look like a professional job as the neighbours had heard no noise.

Mabala Mungo was stabbed twice before being strangled; his wife, Nadia, was raped; and their daughter was locked up in the refrigerator.

Although the house was ransacked, the police ruled out robbery as the housekeeper, Magda Nufi, confirmed that nothing valuable was taken. Mr Mungo was a senior geophysicist at Exxon Tumaranda Inc., and was known for his radical views. His constant trips to the U.S. had been viewed with suspicion. Sources close to his friends believe he has been assassinated for knowing too much about corporate deals.

The public prosecutor and the boys at the 8th Police Precinct are hard at work

on the investigation which, at face value,
is expected to be protracted.

4

For the past few days, the Salami League Party had been organising glitzy pep rallies to shore up its importance. A flame-out had recently occurred in a corporate bank riddled with riddles. In a quick-fix parliamentary system, Tumaranda's M.P. was just a nodding dog. At Paradise Avenue, customers were experiencing fleecing at the hands of restaurateurs. Next to the CMS, want, neglect, and confusion reigned at the district hospital. In a confused moment, many a pyrrhic attempt was made to gag the press.

Amidst all of this, could there be any certitude? Investigative reporter Jason Makelekele of *The Tumaranda Star* found the situation un-heroic and became unduly curious. After panning and fanning through many articles, he thought he had come up with what was supposed to be a tell-all story.

The Tumaranda Star was respected for its unusual political balancing act. In a bottom-line driven profession, it sought ethical and responsible reporting outright. Yet, there was a connective tissue of shared danger. Many unsolved crimes had begun to beg the question of the workability of the justice system. Was there a lead, as the Mabala Mungo affair was becoming a headache for students of homicide cases? Death, be it by suicide, poisoning or murder, stinks high.

*

Bundu Bakasili, Yeelena Theodora and their friend, Jason Makelekele of *The Tumaranda Star*, met for dinner Saturday evening at The Licking

Stick. They had vegetables with stockfish, yams, carrot soup, and shrimps.

Yeelena Theodora wore a necklace of cultured pearls. "Don't you think this investigation for your article can land you in trouble?" she said to Jason.

"Good thing our friend Bakasili here is a police officer," Jason said. "He will bail me out without breaking a sweat."

"I saw that coming," Bakasili cut in with head-nodding interest, "we at homicide don't need journalists sniffing around—"

"Aha!" Theodora quipped and, borrowing a line from George Eliot, added, "A difference of taste in jokes is a great strain on the affectations."

An awkward silence sat between them for a while. From a broad vista, the neon lights of the town seemed to glitter like some space station in a science fiction movie. It was obvious that the threesome had formed a triple helix of common initiative, people ready to take some kind of corrective measure.

Bakasili stroked Theodora's hands, looking her in the eye. "I want us to have serious plans."

She looked up at him. "Do you really love me?"

There was an air-rending silence before any love decisions could be taken. Life at times needed certain compromises.

"Don't let me down," Theodora intoned back in a sing-song manner.

The huzzah reaction from Makelekele did not take long to come. He had only been a passionate observer to the cryptic love oath taking. "I'll send you two presents from afar," Makelekele declared with a wink in the eye.

A Sha-la-la song began humming in the jukebox in the background. Bakasili and Theodora were now locked in a long, passionate kiss.

5

Tumarandan politicians were mimic men—the type history books have been spending time trying to analyse. Forgetting that the art of governing requires that one never give up the initiative of radical element, the people's representatives engaged in disclaimers, anti-confessions, and their ongoing war against the press. The majority of the papers had accumulated sediments of sloganeering and chorus-line headlines as a ruse to avoid attention. Only *The Tumaranda Star* stood firm on the orgiastic coverage of events. Jason Makelekele wrote an opinion piece in its latest issue, speculating that there was a cover-up on the Mungo murders.

*

The Oil Taste Embarrassment
a special
by Jason Makelekele

I have come to the conclusion that the Mabala Mungo murder case, about which much ink has been spilled, is neither a bootless argument nor a prying speculation. It needs an articulate treatment for a swinging generation that is awash with new delights and insight.

Since no one wants to acknowledge pro-forma responsibility for the infamy, the accumulation of riff-raff reports seem more than just a judicial opinion. Why has there been no public outcry against such brazen and violent killings?

Is the Sophoclean intensity not enough for the people's voice to yearn for a minority report? Can we say that a triple murder has no author or authors, or motive? What kind of ancient tribal hunter surge could have led to such gory pornographic violence?

Leaked documents show that higher-ups had knowledge of a certain black market sale of embezzled crude oil to a multi-national. A confidential pamphlet circulating in European capitals talk of the Kasongo Triangle, a triad in apparent mockery of the Bermuda Triangle. How many barrels or is it a tanker load that was involved? Who got what cut? Did the Mungos have to die for others to gain? Now that this information is out in the public, will a fresh enquiry be called on the Mungo File?

*

The news cycles brought a lot of attention to a murdered man who was not a public figure. Mabala Mungo had gotten engineering degrees from two professional schools in the U.S.—the Carnegie Institute of Technology, and the California Institute of Technology. He first worked with Texas Electronics, Houston, before taking up a high-profile job as geologist with AMOCO, Luanda. He was the drilling industry's most valuable asset. After only three years on the Angolan scene, he got hired away under a fabulous contract by Exxon, Tumaranda. As a geophysicist, exploration decisions and sensing analysis brought him untold fortunes. He became a market value man, with a salary running in several digits more than those of his colleagues.

He was on and off in activities both on- and off-shore. He worked ceaselessly using an Altair 8800 computer from which he was hardly separated. There were geophysical surveys, geophone records, core and econometric analyses—he was a hands-on engineer who did catch the envy of many. His murder was the talk of every paper as journalists unearthed every nook and cranny of his past, both real and speculative.

*

Makelekele joined Solo Marie KumKum—a nabob from Ya Salaam—for a smoke at the men's section of Xanadu Resort. Inhaling from the hookah was a distress killer. He found himself drifting into a world that was a sober mix of excitation and kinky fantasy, a swollen ocean full of events.

The club itself was a fount of subversive energy. Radical ideas got a serious hearing. The fault lines had thus been drawn. Two of them had the opinion that something had run amok with the Mungo investigation. In between thin lines of smoke, the twosome spoke out as if under the influence of mescaline.

"The police investigation is a freak show," Makelekele said, his face sweaty. "There is a missing link. Where has the law gone?"

"You are asking a question whose answer is obvious," KumKum said with an awkward laugh.

"Have you ever heard the moans of a man being murdered?"

"Murder can't be that sexy."

"Someone's hands have been bloodied up."

"Please, let's enjoy our smoke, and let sleeping dogs lie," KumKum said, and a soundless tension swelled between them.

6

Tumaranda woke up that mid-September morning to a tropical shower. It did not just rain, it poured; early morning rain was considered a sign of a lousy business day ahead. At midday, Jason Makelekele sat down at his desk at *The Tumaranda Star*'s office, tired and worried. At the other desks, reporters were busy crafting headlines and kickers, revising text, and running fact checks.

Liza, Makelekele's commissioning editor, shouted at him from the other end of the office: "Hey! Mr Pulitzer, where is that your prized story?" Everyone laughed with a little bonhomie.

The paper that day was rich with curious stories about a curious world: an analysis of the various newspaper articles disagreeing with a recent psychologists' seminar that came up with the view that love was dirty; a newly discovered hamlet called Asomara, where girls were still subjected to genital mutilation and forced marriages; an opinion piece arguing that cloning was likely to send metaphysics to the dustbin; an article on filmmakers serving the audience repetitive adventure stories, as if moviegoers were les cochons des payants.

Jason Makelekele reached for the office phone, and dialled Mabala Mungo's younger brother, Tubby, who worked on the other side of town, at a business consultancy.

"Hello?" a voice said.

"This is Makelekele of *The Tumaranda Star*. Is that you, Tubby?"

After a lull, a husky voice came on: "This is Tubby. Can I help you?"

"I need a new lead on that investigation."

"You know that case is a taboo subject and the walls have ears," Tubby said. "I'll help you just this once, and that's it. Contact Domino Osongo of Matrix Insurance. Say I sent you."

The line went dead.

Makelekele was now on a steady path with so many cryptic leads, botched pieces of forensic evidence, foul play, and cover-ups.

*

After two months of false leads, the investigation was still moving at tortoise speed. The Domino Osongo lead was a boon; it led to another lead, Jessica Bantu. Makelekele tracked her down and pretended to bump into her at a record store. They quickly bonded over their love for music and

Makelekele invited her to join him and some friends over the weekend.

Makelekele, Yeelena, Bantu, and Bakasili went to the Tony Muntezuma nightclub one Saturday night in January 1977. The decibel super dome pulsated to the rhythm of rumba, salsa, samba, merengue, cha cha, calypso, and zouk.

While the two men wore casual, trendy clothes, the women were dressed to kill. Jessica Bantu looked demure in a satin dress, and fur coat. Against the background of the neon dazzle, Yeelena Theodora was radiant in a maxi skirt, and a glittering blouse. At a nearby table sat a man wearing a plumed turban.

The club was a pleasure place, where groups of friends could fraternise. But it turned out that their next-table neighbour was a cigar puffing, snobbish, vain, and disrespectful man; the evening was braced up for chewing the odds! But the foursome kept a stiff upper lip, portraying moods of tolerance.

Such a merry company in the hodgepodge of the evening could settle for nothing but bare candour. The music was soothing. Jason Makelekele looked around the room at the people dancing to the beat of the tambourine, and marimba.

Dawn was now only an hour or so away. The peppy dance tunes had been punctuated with a toast to the late night by the disc jockey. Everyone was in a happy mood, glittering in sartorial innovations.

At last, folk wisdom had it that home was the last destination. As the foursome drove home in two separate cars, they enjoyed the night-time dazzle and advertisement boards. An amorous couple passed by. Softly, the girl was humming a Tamla Motown obbligato, "Stop! in the Name of Love."

7

One fine day in March, Makelekele visited the large archives room of the 8th Police Precinct. His friend, Detective Bakasili, had gone on a special assignment to Kabosaga, where a cult famous for human sacrifice had been identified. He had pulled strings before leaving, to make sure that Makelekele had access to the archives of the precinct. The archives room was a labyrinth of cupboards, racks, boxes, paperwork, sealed envelopes, maps, photographs and their negatives, fact files, plastic exhibit bags, and other stuff. The room was stuffy due to a lack of proper ventilation. With his professional touch, he pried through the confidential files. The files, at some point, seemed to turn into some ancient dream, like some cryptic hieroglyphic papyrus scroll.

Makelekele looked through the files in a drawer marked *M*: Makara, Moliki, Mokolo, Mungo. He pulled out a large envelope. It contained pictures of a man lying face down in a pool of blood, and a gagged, murdered woman, and a child in a refrigerator. There was another small envelope with a red tape and broken wax, with the inscription *700/CTS/Condor/Mungo; case to be re-opened after twenty years. Classified!*

Then, there was the piece of paper with an enigmatic, telex-like message:

TEMPLAR IN THELMA UNICORN

TWILIGHT ALPHA/OMNIBUS

OMETTA TEST. YAK OF KEY

TO ELLA. MONTE CARLO.

*

47

A day after that momentous discovery, Makelekele was all worked up. Jessica Bantu had not yet let slip any information, but he was convinced the cryptic message from the documents at the precinct must mean something. A welter of feelings raced through his mind. Was he on the verge of a scoop?

As he slept on Sunday night, little did he know that he would be a voyager of awareness in some astral mumbo-jumbo flight. It was a baroque night full of reveries where the embrace of excess was a wispy blur of the House of Aires. Spiritual seekers and dreamers do have one common denominator—they are whisked into that realm by a torture of the mind. And like a mirror, the reflection comes on convex-like, bending the images and giving it some kind of lurid meaning.

Twilight of Crooks

Makelekele's mind wrestled with myth in a queasy adventure that looked like spooks hunting. There was something gaga here. Soon there came the recurring sound of music—some kind of symphony that opened up a magic mantra. The sound then segued into a rock-rhapsody song, "Psycho Killer" by Talking Heads. No explanation was forthcoming. Makelekele, the dream boy, dreamt on, with a large banner for a finis bearing the words "THE KEY TO ELLA", and with the face of Mabala Mungo crying for salvation.

The dream was confusing.

*

No one knew how the demonstration in Tumaranda had started. Led by Reverend Wilson Manana, over four hundred people, accompanied by dogs and other pets, had got fed up with melancholy truths.

The police broke up the demonstration with unmeasured brutality. They were not mere peacekeeping officers, but warriors with unlimited powers. They showed no mercy to prying pressmen either, since they had vested interests. Not all social animals are social, it has been said, in response to Aristotle. After the crackdown on the demonstrators, the police stormed press offices and seized the day's issues. It almost felt like revenge, because this time around the gun was mightier than the pen.

A week after the incident, a group of reporters met for brunch at Cecilia's Place. All the newspapers were there—*The Vanguard, The Tumaranda Star, The City Voice, Pulse News, 24*

Hours—in all suggestive outfits and demure dresses. This bunch reflected a meeting of the minds, where consciences could explode. With quick ideas, they could see things with more than just a pair of eyes.

At the round table under a crystal chandelier, culinary action was at its best. The food consisted of an African special. Beautiful people ought to eat tasty food. For such a trendy restaurant, the food had had a few touches of condiment excitement. The waitresses with their eye-catching dresses were each competing for the favours of these print media personalities. And the food, exuding exotic aroma, came in a procession. There was; of course, Tumaranda couscous, smoked trout, carrot-cum-cauliflower stew with a shake of pepper and a side dish of sweet peppered mish-mash soup. It was a smash as their culinary aspirations rivalled each other.

While they ate, they spoke little; the food was generating more energy in them. Reporters, in mock ambition, did have differences in political attitudes, yet they all agreed that they had a common enemy—the police—and that they had to work together to stop their abuses of power. Their brainstorm session ended with the sharing of information.

*

Makelekele sat in Sophie Ondo's living room, the large settee engulfing him. It was a serene evening, full of promise. The room was square and seemed to squeeze them into place. Some far-off light streaked in through half-drawn blinds. The atmosphere felt eerily quiet even though the hi-fi system oozed light instrumental music. His conversations with Jessica Bantu had led him to Sophie Ondo.

Sophie Ondo gave him a glass of water and sat opposite him, staring at a painting on the wall. She answered Makelekele's questions, ignorant of the consequences of being a whistle-blower.

She looked pale, and was shaky. Tears tumbled down her cheeks. The laboured patience only went on. It had been a gamble. Lots of money had changed hands and pockets. This had been corruption with a philosophical view: thieves-in-law nexus, conspiracies, shady deals, make-believe, above-the-law. The war between Exxon and Esso could be found in coded messages. Sophie Ondo was Exxon's code breaker, but contrary to protocol, she had brought confidential files home to work on them overnight more than once. The revelations brought traumatic stress.

Ondo pulled out a pack of cigarettes, took one stick, and lit it. She had stopped crying. She leaned back into the settee, took a drag, blew out smoke, then asked, "How bad do you want a copy of a top secret internal memo stating that Mabala Mungo was becoming a problem?"

*

The Tumaranda Star office was a beehive of activity. At his desk, Makelekele had a stack of newspapers from rival presses sitting in front of him. The papers bore every indication that the government was unrepentant following the incident where the police broke up the protest. The headlines were telling.

"TUMARANDA'S PETERLOO, ARE WE
SAFE?"
"TO THE DAY OF ATONEMENT"
"PEACE OFFICERS RUN AMOK"
"TUMARANDA IN SHAMELAND"

The headlines were enough to express the cynical logic of the whole show. Makelekele tried to take his mind away from the newspapers and, just at that moment, he heard footsteps and looked up. Yeelena Theodora was walking into his office.

"To what do I owe this visit?" Makelekele said as he stood up to greet her.

A wide smile played over Theodora's face as her mind espoused many causes. "There are gossiping tongues that say you need some young girlie by your side," Theodora faked humour.

55

Makelekele did not seize the humour. He looked unfazed. Bachelorhood was becoming intolerable. It was a worry. There was a lull.

"Well, there we go again. Can we now talk? As you see, I'm on my way to King Solomon's Mines—Johannesburg—for business." She edged herself towards him with a twinkle in the eye, then hushed as if she were about to reveal some boudoir secrets, and whispered, "Bakasili says you should be careful. Apparently, someone else knows you are in possession of classified documents."

Yeelena left as suddenly as she had arrived. Makelekele was antsy for the rest of the day and did not notice time passing by until he was hungry.

8

Makelekele listened many times and carefully, too, to the promptings of some voices from on high. Here, now, was the time to fathom out the meaning of life. With so many hit men on the run and glorified, the idea of buying a handgun crossed his mind. These things could now be got across the counter everywhere. How was he going to protect himself, or was it going to be tomorrow's vial of anthrax?

In the face of a confused calendar, Makelekele was anxious for a sign. After an hour's brooding that morning, he picked up a recent copy of *Jane's*, and began admiring the latest in Chieftain tanks and attack aircraft gadgetry.

"Hey, can you look at this story before you set out on the prison break investigation?" Liza,

Makelekele's editor, said. Makelekele looked up from the magazine. "That's a bright idea, enlisting me for diversions."

"Your case has become too hot for *The Tumaranda Star*," Liza said, with a faux smile on her face. "We are dropping it. I am under a lot of pressure. Let's talk of recent happenings, not bygones. I've been in this job for long and I want to last. You see, I have a family eh!"

"I see the old hawk is bowing out over the first signs of trouble," Makelekele cut in.

"Let's make peace. Act like an adult," the editor said in a droll voice, refusing to be annoyed. "Remember the old saying: he who pays the piper, calls the tune!"

Twilight of Crooks

"Is this a beggar's opera?" Makelekele questioned back, groping in the borderline mist of annoyance and frustration.

The battle lines were now drawn. Makelekele would not engage himself in rigmarole diversions.

*

The whittling and dreaming of the 70s raced around. There were visible signs that something had to go awry. After that verbal spar with the editor, Makelekele knew that he had spoken without misting up. Pressmen are great finders of faults. Political debate had been skewed, journalists had been ionised, and the public was being fobbed off with lies.

There were clamours for some openness. The opposition parties began to rile. This backlash left the country with a diplomatic black eye. The ruling class was unplugging. With granitic arrogance, the state radio, in all of its monopolistic haste, engaged in impolitic comments describing reform-seekers as "unpatriotic lowlifes imitating some foreign culture". A dangerous level had been reached and insistent denial harboured some explosive potential.

*

A little wind was blowing over Tumaranda; the sky promised huge showers. A crowd gathered in City Hall. Everyone was sweating. They had come to demand that the council restitute their expropriated land. The council had been involved in all sorts of payola—its top crust did boast: "Behold we have made profit; we milked the cow!"

Mayor Yuri Sonni had cut short his lunch to attend to the situation. While addressing the crowd, he kept a respectful distance for fear of having rotten eggs and tomatoes thrown at him. In an arch tone, he rolled out a blithe phrase: "We are conscious of your plight, and the municipal government is doing everything to address the situation," he said. "The scheme is for the good of everyone. Don't listen to gossip."

The crowd was not satisfied with this explanation, and it booed.

Pressmen shot out questions at the Mayor like an inquisition.

"Do bear with me," he said in a kind of concealed haste. "Real estate is an important tool of development. You all will be compensated, depending on available resources."

Despite his efforts, no one could bet a penny on his sincerity.

"Each case will be treated separately," he continued. "We cannot mix beans and groundnuts. Nor are we going to tolerate triad constructions dotted here and there." He was calling the shots.

The rain suddenly poured, as if in disapproval, and the angry crowd dispersed in a depressing au revoir. Later that evening at the Tumaranda City Hall, Mayor Sunni was having a pretty good time. He had just had a phone conversation with the owner of *The Tumaranda Star* about one of his columnists who was sniffing all over town for leads on the Mabala Mungo murder after he had been asked to drop the case. In a no-nonsense mood, he had strong-armed the owner of The Tumaranda Star into taking this issue very seriously. Jason Makelekele was busy writing a story about a new fad: a frog hip dish served at restaurants to shore up virility. With soulful eyes, he re-read the last sentence, which ended with a zinger, and forced out a laugh.

The phone rang. He picked it up, spoke into it, then replaced it in its stand. He made his way to his editor's office.

Without saying a word, she handed him a faxed letter. Makelekele read the message. There was silence.

"This will cool you off for some time, eh?" the editor said, breaking the silence.

Makelekele still could not speak. He had just been asked to travel to Bonn, Germany, as the representative of *The Tumaranda Star*, for a three-month refresher course that was part of a partnership between the newspaper and several German and international media outlets.

9

It was unbelievably cold that November afternoon as the group of Third World reporters checked in at the boisterous Ameron Hotel Königshof on the banks of the Rhine. Outside, a swarm of birds flew up into the grey sky in one move. There were many people in the hotel's lounge and lobby. At the other end of the bar, a couple, probably of Slavic stock, sat in companionable silence.

Jason Makelekele felt odd here. He was confused. He was now far away from that spectre in which fear and trust had been uneasy bedfellows. Bonn was not supposed to sound far-fetched—the values were there, lots of freedom.

Deutschland was to become the new scene of drama for several journalists from different countries who came here for workshops and refresher courses. The check-in list had included reporters from far and wide—*The Managua Times*, *Saint Kitts's Dispatch*, *The Tumaranda Star*, *Soweto Mail*, *Tasmania Chronicle*, *Madras Herald*, and *Kampala Voice*—a variegated lot with differing views, thought, and temperament. Südstadt, where the Communication Institute was located, was a lively neighbourhood. There were the bistros, the spiffy restaurants, flower shops, bookshops and, of course, the banks. A lot of streetwalkers carried faces shrouded in ruse; Germans are cunning, do look self-important, and assert it all the time. Stop. Look. Listen.

Evening came too soon the second day. Makelekele walked out of the hotel and moved along the strasse for a while, his thoughts scurrying back and forth. He went into a bistro. The place had a few customers in it. A Barbra Streisand medley hummed from the speakers. The man at the counter mooded up to one of the songs.

Makelekele was now in the swim, learning and enjoying the German way of life. However, he still felt uneasy about being the only Black in the bistro.

*

The reporters were here to face the challenges of news-gathering, and interviewing people who did not necessarily speak their language. The course was sponsored by the Friedrich Naumann Stiftung. Voices were raised about daily risks taken in environments where governments bossed citizens around. Truth was a bitter pill. Honest folk did not live anymore. However ambitious an investigative report went, however insatiable a reporter ploughed, there was the likelihood that an embargo could meddle. Tout comprendre, c'est tout pardonner!

Awara Abdullah of *Madras Herald* had a point. His government had countered a revealing story on grand-style corruption with a communiqué describing his article as "tittle-tattle of nonsense mired in a succession of speculations and hearsay." This was only the icing on the cake: if everyone revealed their goings-on, it would only open up Pandora's box.

Governments lived with a permanent syndrome of fear. Herr Nikolas Gunter was a senior resource person whose conduct of the meeting of the minds had been rewarding. His career had evolved on a forked complex of ideas and he spoke about his journalistic experiences with spooky accuracy. The question to always ask, he posited, was "have we as yet fulfilled what journalism we have?" The options of courage and daring were a needed feature, and it was not taught in any school.

And so the days raced on.

*

How comforting it was to embark on the last segment of the German stay that smacked of adventures in a travelogue. If Bonn was considered a cool city, it was small beer compared with Frankfurt. Frankfurt's Metropolitan philharmonic orchestra could belt out such a consummate performance of "A 5th of Beethoven" such as to have one drift into Morpheus' arms. And the city's taste for burgundy could swell a fellow.

Köln was the communication city, where the voice of Deutschland went far and wide. With a sudden access of irony, Deutsch Welle, ZDF, and Transtel occupied a dicey position. Munchën was the foam capital, where beer-drinking and traditional dances were major attractions.

Visiting these places had been a snowball chance for everyone. And, in whispers, Makelekele could be heard saying, "Oh, how we had traipsed around; how we had cottoned on to new ideas; how we had made eyes and furtive glances at German belles and received flirtatious replies; how we had enjoyed dervish dances; how we had confronted a brave new world; how we had enjoyed the jingling procession of attendants and fun fair gypsies at the Hanover fest; we… we… enough of that preacher tone. Take your pick!"

But there was a catch somewhere. Across the borders, the West Germans had their blood brothers living in East Germany or GDR, behind the Iron Curtain. Only rumours could tell of what transpired in that communist bastion. There was the Berlin Wall, Berlin's Checkpoint Charlie, the STASI, the Cold War; all looked like fiction. But there was now talk of mutual tolerance and respect, or even Realpolitik.

*

The weeks raced on. Makelekele's head was a tumult of thought and reluctant facts. He had acquired new skills in a region where liberty and democracy made some sense. Nostalgia had begun to set in. The political tedium that prevailed some six thousand kilometres away in Tumaranda was still lurking around.

Awara Abdullah, who caught up with Makelekele at a McDonald's eatery near the Institute, also seemed to be suffering the same kind of journalistic torments.

"I've been in rather good spirits out here," Abdullah confessed as they each sat down at table for a Big Mac, a pack of French fries, a huge mug of iced Coke, and a glass of milk shake. "In India, you are either a chorus boy or you feel the pinch. You didn't need to go far to unpick the assumptions," Abdullah continued.

"This is time for reflection," Makelekele answered back. "I think we are two of a kind".

"Oh, really," Abdullah cut in, his eyes turning hazel and seeming not to be fatally ready.

Abdullah had been raised to have a big city soul. He had grown up in a part of Madras where the gulf between the rich and the poor got constantly wider, where poverty entrenched families. The local state government was either in or out because of the abuse of power or cases of endemic corruption. To have been a reporter in such a society and shied away from those realities would have been like painting a portrait of denial.

"There is something wrong with the Third World," Makelekele suggested amid the jumble of voices from the affable neighbours in the restaurant.

"We are the sacrificial lambs," Abdullah forced out a vexatious declaration as if his throat was choking with emery dust.

"Damned be it," Makelekele, with a little bit of attitudinising, stammered out a cosy thought. "Do you know that my editor is a dangerous patronising elf?" The definition looked like a joke in a charming fashion.

News hounds in tight societies had become hemmed in like Daniel in the lion's den, or was it Jonah in the belly of the whale? These species were everybody's scapegoat, some kind of fodder to be fed to the hogs. Governments were not governing but bossing around. Could the end of bossism come through information's highway?

As they sat musing, a dandelion of light in a strange aspect burst through the Palladian window. John Mwaliamungu of *Kampala Voice* later joined them with greetings in Swahili and a curious smile, taking a seat while the restaurant's TV was screening *The Odessa File*.

*

Twilight of Crooks

An after-weekend party was organised for the reporters by the Burgomaster of Bonn, Herr Gustav Mayer. The group took off time to visit some city hallmarks. At the Bonn National Library, Makelekele got acquainted with the works of dissonant German writers like Herman Hesse, Georg Lukács, and Heinrick Böll. At a private foundation library, he also took resourceful notes on the World War II horror camps of Dachau, Auschwitz, Sobibor, and Treblinka; Schindler's List; the quest for the Holy Grail, Aryan syncretism, and even the story of the capture of Nazi fugitive General Eichmann in Argentina by MOSAD agents.

The German perspective was a proper window. Clichés aside, the insights though interwoven and contradictory led Makelekele to muster much in a wracking moment of decision. Could it be engaging? Reflection in the Galbraithian sense needed introspection and a sense of knowledgeability. He still had to muster attitude to remain true to himself: be alive and kicking, and perhaps ambitious in that spacious world of journalism. But then a voice was crying in that shameless wilderness of impunity. People-watchers had to stand their ground, for they were also being watched as patterns do repeat themselves. Well, God has plans for everyone. All these thoughts came against the backdrop of enjoyable popular TV series with Inspectors Derrick and Körster.

*

It was a long Sunday night and Makelekele seemed to be enjoying the balmy evening breeze filtering into the hotel room. He was in bed feeling sleepy, yet he wanted to play on as if sleep were a game. The relationship between people and sleep is so vital, yet there is no address book to call up a number to indicate whatever kind of sleep you want. Sleep falls within a realm that straddles life and death, and uncertainty. Lady Sleep flashes many distinct and weird, convex memories. If at all there is a dream, it is like the take-off of a plane that soon attains altitude in an exposure of the senses.

And so Makelekele drifted into one of those reverie experiences. Rain poured in that land where he had gone to, like it had never done before. There was a likelihood of a flood. As hours raced on things became unclear. Soon alarm bells and sirens filled the air. Panic ensued as evacuation began in earnest. The water level only rose and rose—ten metres, twenty, twenty-five… Choppers and other flying gadgets were everywhere with searchlights.

A floating procession of rescue boats moved fast. Alas, one queer boat arrived with a difference. It was larger than a ship or even Leviathan and had some mystical bearings about it. A dancing light of such luminance as could almost be likened to the Biblical Noah's ark. Everybody seemed to be boarding it, including Makelekele. Soon, the ark floated away like an eleventh wave and later nested, after the deluge, on a foggy-frosty mountain in Kathmandu. A thousand saffron-robbed monks led by a shaman were in waiting, kow-towing and chanting.

"A thousand years, we have waited."

"What is it that you dream of?" the shaman asked Makelekele matter-of-factly.

"I don't know," Makelekele replied pointedly.

"Who says that you don't know anything," the diminutive man spoke with sublime dazzling simplicity.

"I'm confused," Makelekele responded.

The Shaman looked radiant as if looking through the Mirror of Solomon. He paused for some time before continuing the induction.

"My boy, as you rightly say, you're confused. Confusion is a tricky little subject. Confusion has always been there—alpha, omega. This thing called the Big Bang is just confusion. Confusion created the world. Confusion created rocks, trees, water, and animals. Sin is confusion. Earthquakes, volcanoes, tsunamis, legends, history or even religion, are all confusion!

"Then who are we?" Makelekele, who had been all ears, begged for an answer.

"We're all travellers and sojourners," the old man ventured a reply. "We go and come in an eternal confusion called 're-incarnation'."

The teachings at the foot of the master seemed endless. And the dream came and went like a sensation. When he woke up to a bright day the following morning, he felt rather catatonic. Such was the fountain of surprises that had come to Makelekele in the name of a revolving circle in a flight of fancy!

10

Two weeks more, and the course would come to an end. That Saturday evening back in Bonn, the sky was bathed in stars. Makelekele and three other reporters walked up and strolled down three streets just to light up their farewell performances. The outing was meant to outsource their emotional needs during the nervous moments before departure. The night was cold and icicles hung from trees, twinkling like tiny stars. Traffic warmed up, cars raced in various directions.

In his hind mind, Makelekele was eager to be home in Tumaranda. He wanted to write one last article about the Mabala Mungo murder. He had gathered so much new information before he left Tumaranda and he was more confident than ever. He would quit *The Tumaranda Star* and find a suitable home for the article, which had high-decibel allegations. Perhaps it could earn him the Congo Star Award in journalism.

The group of reporters stopped in front of a bookshop. Posters on the exterior glass wall panel announced that Günter Grass and Herman Hesse had new novels out.

Yet there was nothing they had to be bashful about.

They were really hungry. They chose a restaurant at random. A German couple with golden hair sat at the table across from the reporters. Light music, probably Klaus Wunderlich, filled the air. At the seats near the window, they could see a Marks and Spencer; the building's design resembled a tomb without the gloom.

"Bon appétit!" said the waiter.

Alone in his hotel room later that night, Makelekele ransacked his briefcase and brought out some scraps of paper with notes he had taken for an article he was writing.

The following day, the reporters took a series of end-of-course lectures in mass media in a cinema and television world. As could be seen, these two subjects followed people all around. Both newspapers and TV stations had to uplift or even debunk the assumption that audiences or readers did take for granted what they saw or read. Terrorism was a new appeal subject with its reporting often bogged down by official statements; should fire be answered with fire and should terrorists be terrorised? Then came the arts, begging to be reported as an instrument of social change while development journalism evolved on the knowledgeability of reporters, which was put to question and, of course, the "for whom the bell tolls" nuance.

These insights only emboldened Makelekele's resolve to brace up for the cause at the home front. What were the choices? How jolly and committed the other reporters sounded too. Every country had its own sins proportioned to its reproach. Which then would be the bits that some people may not want to swallow? This is where Third World reporters stand between the hammer and the anvil, with political cynicism showing its ugly Hydra-head in the horizon. The course had come to an end and it was time to return to Tumaranda.

11

The Tumaranda embassy in suburban Bonn was a compact building that had been chosen because of budgetary constraints. The white flag floating in front of the stone-and-granite building was bright, with a mango at its centre. The entrance to the embassy had a mini arch of triumph that opened up to twenty-something steps, which ended in front of an iron, theft-proof door two times a man's height. Conspicuous was the blue beeper to announce visitors and, in gold letters, was the inscription 'Embassy of Tumaranda'.

As Makelekele approached the embassy, he moved with an air of confidence.

The embassy door opened to reveal a smiling woman welcoming him. The building's interior was a constellation of mural paintings, vases with flora of tropical rainbow eruptions and a life-size sepia portrait of Tumaranda strongman Nikita Mangope. The wait in the waiting room seemed eternal. To kill time, he leafed through the Tumarandan newspapers on the table in front of him.

Back in Tumaranda, newspapers, though still gagged, had lots of things to write about: gang-bangers on the run; tourism to the shuttered houses; the appointment of a certain name-dropper as ambassador; and Tumaranda's top musician, Toledo Kassala, whose new brand rhythm—sambarengue—ascended on spirals of joy. The Mabala Mungo murder investigation was not mentioned by any paper.

He was ushered into the consular office. The official who received Makelekele took two rapid-fire puffs from his cigarette before opening up to conversation. He introduced himself as Johnston Dimabola, the consular officer.

In front of him was a file, which he opened with priestly care.

"Sorry, sir... your return visa has been rejected," the official stammered. The words came out like a knell.

"Really?" Makelekele questioned, registering the statement with pained disbelief.

"He who pays the piper calls the tune," the official, in a mock cliché, announced the stakes unabashedly with a conspirational smile.

"Are you serious?" Makelekele questioned, then added, "I invoke my right of return!"

The diplomat cocked his head and said flatly, "Where do you think you are? We are done here.

You don't believe me? Just as eggs are eggs, so be it."

"But on which side do you break eggs before frying," Makelekele said, trying to humour the situation.

The official looked unfazed. "Can't you see where I'm getting at?" he stammered out.

"If you say so," Makelekele answered back in gentlemanly fashion. "But can I get back my passport?"

Both eyed each other in a veritable clash of vision, ending up with each having a silent x-ray assessment of the other. The battle lines had been drawn. Bonhomie and intelligence had no place here. Makelekele's expression grew pained and hardened. He was finding it impossible to get up from the consular chair. He looked petrified, some kind of being cast in mould magma. Every fibre of his body was shaking.

"I demand to see the ambassador," Makelekele intoned in a harsh voice.

The official chuckled and, with a mocking laugh, pressed on the buzzer and called for security in a groggy voice.

Makelekele was evicted from his own embassy, or territory. He was now an unperson, soon to become a stateless person in quest of nationality. Stuff like that. Beast of no nation. Cooked. Done in. This was a little de trop.

What weighty news. The embassy's line of thought had been lit by a single matrix window. There was nary any one on sight to be of any help. If there was a God, one and three, then this situation was enough to make Makelekele want to eat his own balls. Where then could he work for chains of association!

*

On the way out, Makelekele's thoughts went on rampage.

The problem about fate is that it is tricky and unpredictable. And God said "Let Makelekele be" and lo, he was born with the map of his life traced beforehand. Some palmist will say they can see one's life spread before him. Even the Tarot cards can predict it. The beat was on. It was like Isaac Newton sitting under that apple tree and watching an apple fall down, not up. Many ideas ran through Makelekele's mind, ending up with relativity and fate.

What was related here? The local Tumaranda magician, D.D. Mbah, used to boast that his conjuring feats were the result of his mastery of *The Seven Books of Moses* and *The Book of Dee Lawrence*. This is true to its type, for magical moments can be remembered a thousand times over. Whose side was logic on? Action had been stymied. This was a gamble and fate was full of gambles. How indulgent this view can be. A man on the murky road of fate had to keep afloat and moon around. The lines to walk could be fraught with traps. And this can be done with the assumption that other people mind their own business. He kept walking, for it was not the end.

Do yourself a favour as one mirrors self. Whom do you see? Fate appears again. It is the tool of the creator and, is one to question its wherefore in the depths of self?

This jumbled zone is a hollowed façade with many corridors and mirrors. The visual connections represent the passage of time. Choices are made—emotional and unemotional—by outside forces not content of acting alone. It always works, for fate incarnates the Alpha and the Omega. In Tumarandan Eyes, fate had become fiction since They had seen too much evil triumph They were frightened by any expectations. Fate toys with family separation and only the victims know the inner turmoil. There is no misreading that. Who wants a breakdown of the soul? This is an embarrassing matrix fashioned into a cosmological metaphor.

These musings only cast Makelekele into the maw of the situation. It was a grand circus, a travesty and a tedium all put into a basket of woes.

Great expectations had become alloyed news. This was him now as a child of two worlds experiencing a kind of methistemi, or social transformation, in an end-game that was proving to be une leçon par la suite. In the fleeting moment, his mind was just throwing ideas around as he relaxed his tired old bones. Heavy sarcasm though!

The downside is that he was edgy or even pissed off. He could not understand why the words 'banished' and 'vanished' kept playing in his mind with some asperity. He heard himself, in a helpless expression, say to those voices: *speak to me*. Was he summoning his karma in this endurance game? Could prayer come in belatedly as a solace?

*

Given the words of the ageless sage, Makelekele knew he was now a sacrificial lamb. There was no fear of transgression as everything was now questioning all he believed in. Fear was a mechanical instrument even though he tried to listen through the doors of a coward's lie. Dreams too tended to be dished out at random and no two people could dream the same story. His psyche was upset, yet this was no time for editorialising. So, at this moment removed in time, he had to walk the primrose path as a feeble semblance of a hazy afternoon was emerging.

In the irony of language, the present situation was proving that fate too could be manipulative, or even a little bit biased. It was just letting the sparks fly. And flight, to or away from, had departure and destination points. What fantasy or even merry-go-round freak show was this that a human being wanted answers? As of now, no earthly instance could prompt a probe into the workings of fate and even hold court before the esplanade of the obelisk of Luxor. In this fleeting astral moment, Zeus and Hera in council at Mount Olympus summoned fate for a hearing!

12

As Makelekele landed on the brick-tiled pavement in front of the Tumarandan embassy, a heavily perfumed white girl came strolling by, dressed in a black skirt, donning an elegant coif and a T-shirt with the words 'Make Love Not War'. This petite girl looked on and exclaimed "What a man!"

On the other side of the street, a wall carried two large posters. One was of French singer Charles Aznavour, announcing a series of international concerts—some tabloids had featured stories of him giving all the wrong reasons why he should be an international star. The other poster was of a new James Bond film starring Roger Moore and Yaphet Kotto.

Time seemed to slow down. Makelekele looked up at the girl. Many things raced in his mind. Time stopped. He smiled. He was thankful there were no German polizei on sight to arrest him for trespassing at the embassy.

The Tumarandan crooks had refused to fold—they were having a glorious twilight and Makelekele, like the Marathon Man, was now to be a runner who would not breast the tape. The criminalisation of the state had thus been consecrated in a state-of-art fashion. All of this had come to be nothing more than a striking reminder of a Chinese triad movie he had once seen, *Duel of Fists*, starring David Chiang and Ti Lung.

True feelings have no one to blurt to. The situation had clearly become a Salman Rushdie sacrificial exit to the whole conspiracy. All was now a je ne sais quoi matter. Since a contrarian was not welcome in his hometown, it was now goodbye to the ersatz of a place called Tumaranda. He now had a wrecked psyche as he hailed a taxi for the hotel. There is no news like bad, sad, mad news.

*

On his way past other pedestrians with their own problems, Makelekele laughed in silly confusion. He fell short of le mot juste in this contre-temps as he found himself swaying in the nebula of a lost generation. To the bastards, conscience was a luxury. His destiny was now a curious thing as fashioned out by that harlot administration. All the signs were showing that he needed a Plan B for survival.

Violence had been used as policy and negotiating tool. Who could not feel and lament, crying for salvation for his beloved country? He flagged down a taxi.

Twilight of Crooks

Through sketches of a panicked conversation with the taxi driver, Makelekele-the-expendable thought of a bottle of large Guinness that could bring back spiritual peace to a wanderer and conjure up his essence.

The rather young taxi driver of Nigerian descent had looked into the mirror and seen Makelekele's over-wrought face. He broke the silence.

"Say, brother, why are you worried?" the driver asked.

"It's... a curious story," Makelekele stammered out a reply. "How can I put it? I'm zonked out and left in the cold. I've been given a new role."

"Are you an actor?" the driver enquired.

"Hell yes, for a new movie scripted in Tumaranda," Makelekele replied, not knowing what was controlling his mind. "The movie is called Exile. Can you see the point?"

"The movie then must be very serious to be done in Germany," the driver complimented. "You must be paid handsomely. We drivers are only on the edge. I left Nigeria for Bonn to experience greener pastures. I was a teacher and here am I as a cab driver in the white man's land."

There was a moment of silence. Both spoke in their hearts. Many kinds of meanings could be inferred. There was a time when the world looked all forlorn, with citizens asking themselves why they were born in such and such a place and not another.

"The truth is, I've become a political refugee," Makelekele tried to explain. "I no longer have a passport. I'm a citizen of nowhere just trying to reach his hotel."

As the driver tried to digest the hidden meaning of what was said, he veered the cab roughly on a last bend to the Imperial Hotel. The afternoon's atmospheric light had become monochrome with a slight rain announcing itself.

13

Back in Tumaranda, a war had been declared on the press as the powers that be tried to silence articles about Makelekele's plight. The emotion captured here was reminiscent of old rivalries—the first versus the fourth estate. In the central conundrum of power, politicians spewed venomous rhetoric at one another. Volcanoes of opinions raced around and begged for anecdotal clarity. The powers that be had made a win with the crucifixion of Makelekele and silenced the fallout, at least in Tumaranda. This was easy because Tumaranda's media culture was under the median with chorus boys constantly jockeying for private advantage.

On his last night at the hotel—his stay had been extended by a few days given the circumstances—Makelekele remembered how, many years ago, he sat on his tatami-mat floor in Tumaranda thinking of how his future as a journalist could be. There had been lines of tremendous curiosity about this 'best profession in the world'. Think of Walter Cronkite of CBS, Stephen Spender of *The Encounter*, Peter Pan Enaharo of *Africa Magazine* or Ako Aya of *Outlook*. These people had been real heroes and purveyors of thought.

Here was the time when the evil genius was at work. It was fashionable for journalists to become scatterbrains, or even janglers of ideas, and pussyfoot around. The calling to the profession was dead. There was a time when parents sang into the ears of their children to tune towards being a lawyer, banker, accountant or taxation official. No wonder Jesus Christ chose, as one of his first companions, a tax collector!

Gone then were the good days. There was always a shadow cast over a reporter in the tropics. Recurring doubts and nightmares became fashionable. Occasionally, a reporter took a dare, with the obvious consequences. However, that harum-scarum quality most recognised in journalists has always been their gift. It is no embarrassing mistake. Come on; appreciate the dilemma and clichés that surround that kind of power. Political carrion-eaters are you men enough!

Makelekele's soft voice could be heard singing in the wind, as he tried to stop his thoughts from wandering…

Twilight of Crooks

Come O spirit of old
Enlighten me, give me courage
Let me accept the task ahead.

Come O guardian angel
Lead me on the path of the brave
Like our ancestors of gone memories

Come O fate and let me rise
Up to that horizon of truth
And be of a brave new dawn!

And so it came to pass in this new state of alertness and awakening… *you are not alone!*

Like Napoleon Bonaparte in exile on the island of Saint Helena, Makelekele looked at the

dark German sky and, in introspection, there came
these pitying questions to the Goddess of Silence:

Who wanted exile and safari?

Who wanted a heart when it can be broken?

Who wanted both ways when only one way was

workable,

Who cares if there is a purpose in this sweaty contest?

Who cares about a bootless argument?

Mock me then.

A burst of lightning shattered this vision as
Makelekele ducked for cover at the hotel's lobby.
It was as if he heard the Goddess laugh, and laugh,
and laugh!

14

On 27 January, Germany was thrown into a world crisis. The Red Army Faction (RAF), a notorious terrorist group, kidnapped German Industrialist Hans Otto Bernhard, and not without violence, killing three family members. The news was all over the airwaves. A statement by the terrorists indicated that their action was in retaliation for its three militants killed by Israeli commandos at Entebbe airport in Uganda. The militants had lent know-how to Palestinian Liberation Organisation (PLO) hijackers in the botched operation the previous year. There were no demands from the terrorists. In this catch-me-who-can game, Germans had spilt German blood. The German government had thus entered into a crisis with the soul-searching statement "we are not weak".

The following day, the German press got ugly with the situation as the terrorists started seeking sensation. Another communiqué from the terrorists with the pronouncement "we are the new light" only portrayed them as a light gone dark. The press could not be impressed. Peace and prosperity could not be shattered by a few anarchists in the pay of communism. The press amplified stories of the Red Army Faction's ties with the Irish Republican Army (IRA), the Red Brigade in Italy, and Libyan strongman Muammar al-Qaddafi.

A cabinet meeting took a tougher stand on this war of wills. There was public fear that there may soon be collateral damage. Chancellor Helmut Kohl spoke for two hours on the phone with his Israeli counterpart, Prime Minister Golda

Meir. The Israelis were known to be efficacious in dealing with terrorists. The Entebbe raid in July the previous year had been an example.

*

Several journalists, both German and foreign, decided they would take the bull by the horns: they would call a press conference the following week, where they would expose Tumaranda's agenda of shame. Makelekele's case was thus beginning to affect diplomatic relations between Tumaranda and Germany. Despite the cold winter, Makelekele was in warm spirits.

These journalists, who had strategised and got the full import of the situation, were now preparing the press conference. This forum was intended to elicit sympathy for a muzzled Third World press and expose the wariness surrounding the forceful exile of reporters by rogue states. They had to burst out their compressed fury and present an instant disqualifier for the men in Tumaranda.

Makelekele, through contingency measures, had been lodged at one of the foundation's rest houses under a political refugee status. The present situation could happen to either one of them at any time.

This new cocoon for Makelekele opened up a spirit of optimism in a place where things were happening. It flashed in his mind that he was a refugee in spite of appearances.

Awara Abdullah, who had extended his stay after the workshop by a few days, caught up with Makelekele for a farewell drink at Bluebird snack-bar just opposite a Japanese sushi restaurant.

"So this is goodbye, I guess," Makelekele said.

"The others and I are still with you in our hearts," Abdullah answered.

"I'll miss all of you dearly, brothers," Makelekele said.

"Now let's take a toast," Abdullah suggested to his friend, whose face was a jumble of worries. "Brighten up; we're not at a funeral."

They both took up their 33 cl bottles and clinked. Of course, Makelekele was brightening up with a Heineken, and Abdullah with a 7up.

*

Saturday morning, just before noon, the press conference took place at the conference room of the Imperial Hotel. A sizeable segment of the media was around. The spokesperson for the journalists was Cruz Castillo of *The Managua*

Times. He took a hard look around the room, and spoke.

"A grave injustice has happened," he began. "Our colleague, Jason Makelekele, of *The Tumaranda Star*, has been made a persona non grata; his country has marooned him in Bonn as if he were a plague! Every time Third World journalists have performed their duties by doing reports that are accurate, balanced and displaying high levels of objectivity, they have incurred the wrath of authorities. Authorities want stories that paint them white, not black. They prevent journalists from attaining sources of information, and even blacklist them." He concluded by urging the German authorities to do something to salvage Jason Makelekele.

*

Twilight of Crooks

Bonn's hofgarten that Saturday afternoon was a mixture of people, especially kids, out enjoying the weekend. At a lake nearby, a couple of children were feeding some gracious swans, to the admiration of their parents sitting on park benches. Other people, mostly elderly, were walking their dogs. The sun was average for this minor winter day. A plane flew above. Other children, with their parents, were flying kites of various colours. There was uniformed polizei.

At the foreign ministry, a press conference was underway, revealing the government's contingency plan for the Red Army Faction hostage crisis. Foreign Minister Klaus Steinbruk was firm and tense: "Terrorism is too demanding for mass acceptance." He paused. "We will not negotiate with terrorists." The tone of the press conference moved on that level while sizing the cold realities and realism of the situation.

As was expected, nothing could be said about the manoeuvres by the anti-terrorism units of the German Black Berets. Or even what had been the result of concertation with Israel and Britain. There is a saying that if you want to eat with the devil, use a long spoon. It was no joking matter, for the mindscape of terrorists was devilish.

15

Jason Makelekele woke up with a start on Wednesday morning. Grey rays of light had penetrated the blinds and given a murky colour to the room. He turned around on the rumpled bed and put on the bedside radio. Radio Free Europe bounced on with a lively DJ hosting on the fifth anniversary of the death of American music prodigy, Otis Redding. The rock song "Nobody's Fault But Mine" was ringing out with such soul vibration.

A scheduled honour concert was announced for the weekend at New York's Apollo Theatre, Harlem. It would feature legends like Ray Charles, Junior Walker, James Brown, Aretha Franklin, Wilson Pickett, Rufus Thomas, Diana Ross,

Smokey Robinson, Clarance Carter, and Gloria Gaynor.

He got up, brushed his teeth and put on after-shave spray sharing spray as he looked at himself in the mirror. There was no mask left to hide behind. The stigma of a sans domicile fixe hung over him. He had to start learning the German language in order to get around. If he had to think back, reminisces abounded. One's dream was one's fate and one, therefore, had to be ready to accept the inevitable. A life without liberty was not worth its salt and, here, there were lots of liberties. He went out and had a light breakfast of orange juice, croissant, and coffee at a mini-restaurant named Arizona, owned by an American expatriate. The calories thus armed him for the day.

Twilight of Crooks

He returned home and decided to nourish his mind with a book he had borrowed from the library on Friedrich Schiller, a thinker, poet, and dramatist, who was often was usually referred to as the German Shakespeare.

*

One too many times during the week that followed, he had taken up a passion for strolling in the Turkish- and Indian-inhabited neighbourhoods of Bonn. They had brought along their cultures and were impacting others. In the past few years, the neighbourhoods had gentrified, especially with fortune-tellers, restaurants, saunas, and cinema halls. One of the façades of Roxi Cinema had one large poster announcing the weekend's Hindi language film, *Aya Toofan*, starring the legendary Dara Singh and KumKum.

Makelekele studied the posters with amused interest.

During the early part of his childhood, Indians had always had large departmental stores in his hometown. There was a myth spreading around about them. Why were these people professed vegetarians? There were rumours that their stores had no bank accounts, that the managers would burn the money taken in, then it would reappear in India. India was, thus, a place of magic and fairy tale.

Makelekele turned around with a bleached smile and understood why he was getting closer to this Indian attraction. His Indian reporter friend, Awara Abdullah, came back to his mind. Yes, he was now back in Madras with a new style of play for his newspaper, *Madras Herald*. Makelekele stood his ground and made a point to watch the movies over the weekend.

It was late afternoon. His steps were heavy as he headed home. A brat on roller skates sporting a portable cassette tape player and headphones bumped into him. That was life. He moved on sluggishly while his head registered some weariness. Near a hardware store on Strasse 22, there was a refuse dump whose contents had overflown. Makelekele was intrigued and pondered why the refuse van had been late for its collection given the state of cleanliness of the city of Bonn. On top of the refuse was an abandoned brown satchel—very inviting. He made a quick judgment call, as if guided by a spirit, and went for the bag. The stench was already climbing high. Amid the rut, flies, maggots, ants, worms, millipedes, and cockroaches were enjoying a holiday habitat, each minding its own business. A dog barked and he turned. It made some futile attempts at climbing the rubber wall of the dump. A bird or two flew down, landed, and pecked a little, catching a worm or two before flying away. What a biological laboratory whose experiments had no researchers!

He reached out and pulled the bag, grateful for his long hands, then moved a little distance away to discover its contents. None of the streetwalkers cared a fig about a black man rummaging through a refuse dump. He opened the satchel and found many sheets of paper with handwritten manuscripts soiled by putrefaction. The manuscripts had marks and indented remarks akin to those of a proofreader. His heart beat faster. He shut the satchel and took it home to discover the magic.

*

The Journal of Jacobo Mann

... as translated by Gustav Atka, a student of *Clio*, one of the nine Muses.

I never thought of going anywhere since I was shot. I was dead. Death was just the beginning, for I found myself convalescing at a weird veterinarian's operating table. Silence was a good cure and a reliable friend. Since then, never heard, never seen. I became a cipher. No tangles on specifics.

But let me start from the beginning. I'm the mystery third man of the famous Bonnie and Clyde heist. More than curiosity will grip anyone who happens upon these manuscripts. I don't intend to excite a tear or two from anyone. Save it.

Any human being has good and bad points. My good point is that I'm tired of being in hiding for the past four years. What is the stuff that dreams and ambition are made of?

The conundrum therefore falls in line with aspirations of civilisations—waiting for someone of action. My hiding has been a parable. And since no one wanted me as a saviour, my time is spent and wasted. I'm bored about my seminal achievement— never being caught. I've watched the establishment; they are sacrificial and restless. Suffice that you give them a headworker. Oh, how they go by the rules of the book. I've always been more than thirty minutes ahead of police thinking. I honour those cold case boys but, unfortunately, they couldn't have recruited such a talent like me. What a loss to miss such an undeniable asset. I have the right to participate in the making of history because I created my own logical and loyal security wall. To win, you must merit. We are cross-armed opposites.

Where then is part of the booty, cache or stash? Herein lies the problem. It's now a game of chess. Moves and counter moves. I used to wonder whatever moved in Bobby Fisher's mind. Such a genius. I'm jealous. But then, money is as money does. Has the Mark been devaluated because I took a few stacks of legal tender that can't be traced? Have the English ever solved the 'great train robbery'?

The hype is beginning to simmer down. I'm not mothballing myself, but I plan to disappear for good, abracadabra. I leave you with the nuanced understanding of no hurt feelings. What was it that surrounded Aesop's fables? "Ich gab mich gefangen," I succumb to his touch!

Enigma, I don't believe in handouts or political omelettes, etcetera, etcetera, etcetera!

*

Makelekele was at a smart and cosy restaurant, Chez Fred, for lunch. It was a busy hangout for foreigners who saw it as a choice trendsetter. A waiter came towards Makelekele and placed a tray of what he had ordered in front of him. He read her name on her breast pocket: Angelika.

The TV was on, showing *The Maltese Falcon*, the chief character's American accent making it difficult for Makelekele to catch a word. After about ten minutes, the movie was interrupted with breaking news: the German Black Beret commandos had, early that morning, put an end to the three-week-old hostage crisis; four Red Army Faction terrorists were gunned down in the pre-dawn raid, which had happened in a warehouse at the former Munich railway station;

the industrialist, Hans Otto Bernhard, was safe, but suffering from post-traumatic stress.

There was a cut to the Foreign Minister. "I appeal for general calm. The German government will never negotiate with terrorists. They are cankerworms and degenerates who must be eradicated even down to sleeper cells. Reliable information indicates that there is an eye of suspicion of complicity from East Germany and Bulgaria."

The story was still developing.

The Maltese Falcon came back on.

EPILOGUE

A month later, Makelekele was still a resident of the Foundation Rest House. It was a rather restless afternoon and he had all the time ahead of him. He was at home. Radio Free Europe was vibrating with American humourist Jerry Lewis, who was spitting out gags for laughs, as part of his European tour. "Jerry be good," the announcer said. Makelekele went out and sat on a chair at the balcony to kill time reading the previous day's issue of the *International Herald Tribune* he had borrowed from the lobby. The paper itself was a copious exercise in view of its size and number of pages. On page 5, he spotted an interesting story.

*

Tumaranda Gets the Heat
UPI-Special Correspondent, Moses Udu

A group of European countries today informed the Tumaranda authorities that it is in the line of fire with prospects of economic sanctions in view of repeated reports of oil scandals, endemic corruption, and absence of good governance.

Reports confirmed by human rights and civil society organisations say that the Tumarandan government had undertaken systematic exercises of harassing the press, organising forceful exiles for citizens it deemed radical, and excelled in lack of transparency.

Certain Foreign Ministries have affirmed that they are reviewing several cases of Tumaranda embassies refusing return visas to its own citizens and tossing them like jetsam. That government has been warned that the mesh can catch fire if this flaunting of power continues.

127

Furthermore, there are signs that the country risks being branded a rogue state.

Tumaranda embassy officials in some European countries have kept a tight upper lip on this diplomatic debacle and carried on business as usual...

*

No comment from Makelekele, who considered the author to have achieved one-upmanship over him. In his mind, a war was now on, pitting socially responsible journalism versus the Spin Doctor's Club in Tumaranda. His eyes moved on to page 40 and something caught his attention in the classified section. In a small box was the message:

Looking for lost bag; contains manuscripts of Jacobo. Handsome reward. Discretion needed. Flat H3253119 Bonn.

128

Makelekele gave off a long smile and seemed to be enjoying his inner ascetic life, which called for this one-liner, "Ich bin ein Bonner". What a silky nuance. Spring was only a few weeks ahead!

Radio Free Europe came on again loud with the hit single, "Ring My Bell", by Anita Ward. Makelekele chuckled and, by that stroke, gained back his sense of humour. What an angel of innocence!

Mwalimu Johnnie MacViban is a senior journalist and news analyst who has worked with the Cameroon Radio Television (CRTV) and *Cameroon Tribune*. He was winner of the 1994 Editor's Choice Award for Poetry by the US National Library of Poetry and his novel, *A Ripple from Abakwa,* was shortlisted for the 2008 EduArt Jane and Rufus Blanchard Award for Fiction. His other books include *An Anecdoted Patchwork, The Makuru Alternative*, and *The Mwalimu's Reader.*

Printed in the United States
by Baker & Taylor Publisher Services